GOSCINNY AND UDERZO
PRESENT
AN ASTERIX ADVENTURE

ASTERIX
AND THE
GREAT DIVIDE

WRITTEN AND ILLUSTRATED BY UDERZO
TRANSLATED BY ANTHEA BELL AND DEREK HOCKRIDGE

HODDER AND STOUGHTON

LONDON   SYDNEY   AUCKLAND   TORONTO

ALREADY PUBLISHED BY HODDER DARGAUD

British Library Cataloguing in Publication Data

Goscinny, René
  Asterix and the great divide.
  I. Title   II. Uderzo, Albert
741.5′944   PN6747

© **Editions Albert René, Goscinny & Uderzo, 1980**

English language text copyright © 1981 by Hodder & Stoughton Ltd
& Editions Albert René, Goscinny & Uderzo,
First published in Great Britain 1981 (cased)
Second impression 1981

First published in Great Britain 1982 (paperbound)

ISBN 0 340 25988 4 (cased)
ISBN 0 340 27627 4 (paperbound)

Printed in Belgium for Hodder & Stoughton Children's Books,
a division of Hodder & Stoughton Ltd
Mill Road, Dunton Green, Sevenoaks, Kent TN13 2YJ
by Henri Proost & Cie, Turnhout

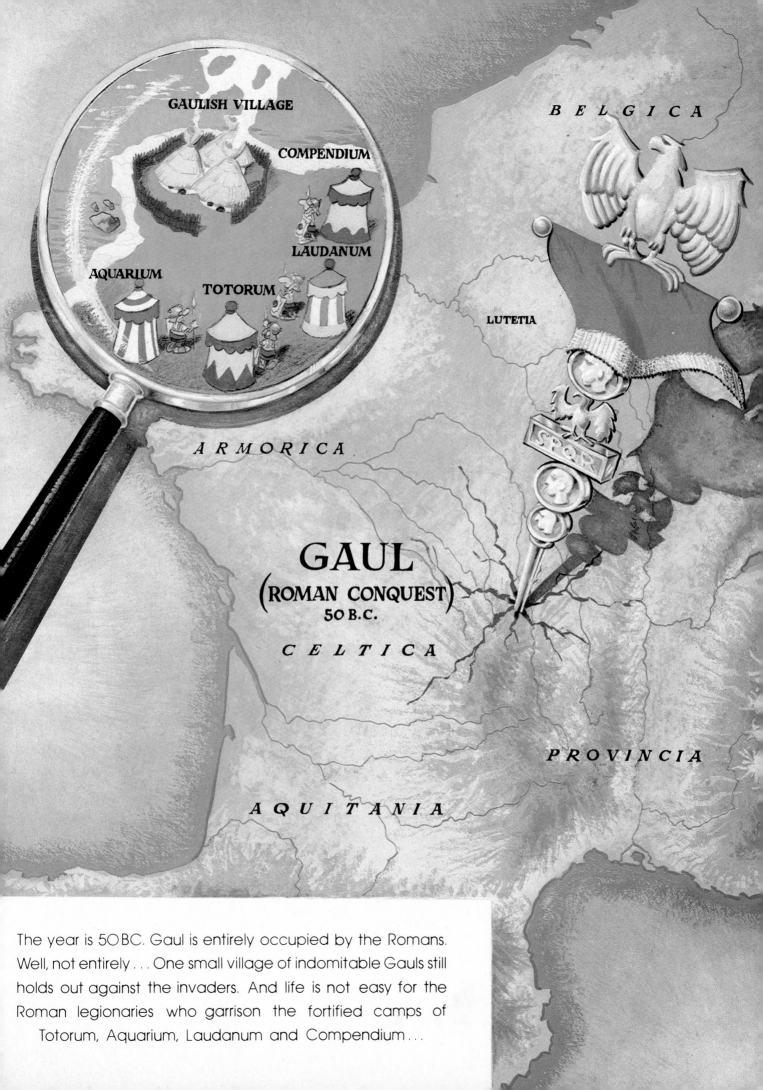

The year is 50 BC. Gaul is entirely occupied by the Romans. Well, not entirely... One small village of indomitable Gauls still holds out against the invaders. And life is not easy for the Roman legionaries who garrison the fortified camps of Totorum, Aquarium, Laudanum and Compendium...

a few of the Gauls

Asterix, the hero of these adventures. A shrewd, cunning little warrior; all perilous missions are immediately entrusted to him. Asterix gets his superhuman strength from the magic potion brewed by the druid Getafix...

Obelix, Asterix's inseparable friend. A menhir delivery-man by trade; addicted to wild boar. Obelix is always ready to drop everything and go off on a new adventure with Asterix – so long as there's wild boar to eat, and plenty of fighting. His constant companion is Dogmatix, the only known canine ecologist, who howls with despair when a tree is cut down.

Getafix, the venerable village druid. Gathers mistletoe and brews magic potions. His speciality is the potion which gives the drinker superhuman strength. But Getafix also has other recipes up his sleeve...

Cacofonix, the bard. Opinion is divided as to his musical gifts. Cacofonix thinks he's a genius. Everyone else thinks he's unspeakable. But so long as he doesn't speak, let alone sing, everybody likes him...

Finally, Vitalstatistix, the chief of the tribe. Majestic, brave and hot-tempered, the old warrior is respected by his men and feared by his enemies. Vitalstatistix himself has only one fear; he is afraid the sky may fall on his head tomorrow. But as he always says, 'Tomorrow never comes.'

SOMEWHERE IN GAUL, PEACE WOULD BE REIGNING IN A LITTLE VILLAGE VERY LIKE THE VILLAGE WHERE ASTERIX LIVES...

...BUT FOR VARIOUS PECULIAR INCIDENTS. A BIG DITCH HAS BEEN DUG THROUGH THE MIDDLE OF THE VILLAGE, SO THAT NO ONE CAN GET FROM THE RIGHT SIDE TO THE LEFT SIDE.

CLEVERDIX HAS BEEN ELECTED CHIEF BY THE LEFT OF THE VILLAGE...

NEVER MIND WHAT THE OTHER LOT SAY, I'VE BEEN UNANIMOUSLY ELECTED VILLAGE CHIEF!

MAJESTIX HAS BEEN ELECTED CHIEF BY THE RIGHT OF THE VILLAGE...MONARCH OF HALF HE SURVEYS.

BY DIVINE RIGHT!

①

5

VARIOUS ATTEMPTS HAVE BEEN MADE TO DEAL WITH THE SITUATION...

AND THE VILLAGERS OF THE LEFT AND THE RIGHT ARE EVER READY TO EXPRESS THEIR MUTUAL ANTAGONISM.

RSPRR! RSPRRR!

BUT IT WOULD TAKE POSITIVELY SINISTER DEXTERITY TO SOLVE CERTAIN VITAL PROBLEMS...

?!

?!

...AND ONLY THE CHILDREN ARE ANY BETTER OFF FOR THE RIFT.

SCRUNCH!

YOU'VE GOT NO RIGHT TO DO THAT! THAT'S MY TREE!!!

SOME OF THE VILLAGERS, HAVING OPTED FOR NEUTRALITY, FIND THAT IT HAS ITS DISADVANTAGES.

DINNER'S READY!

COMING, DARLING!

BONK!

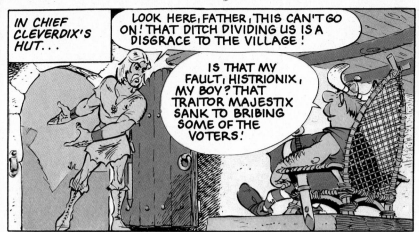

IN CHIEF CLEVERDIX'S HUT...

LOOK HERE, FATHER, THIS CAN'T GO ON! THAT DITCH DIVIDING US IS A DISGRACE TO THE VILLAGE!

IS THAT MY FAULT, HISTRIONIX, MY BOY? THAT TRAITOR MAJESTIX SANK TO BRIBING SOME OF THE VOTERS!

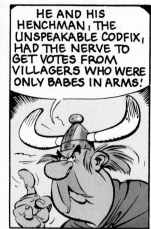

HE AND HIS HENCHMAN, THE UNSPEAKABLE CODFIX, HAD THE NERVE TO GET VOTES FROM VILLAGERS WHO WERE ONLY BABES IN ARMS!

WELL, AT THIS RATE FUTURE GENERATIONS OF GAULS AREN'T GOING TO THINK MUCH OF THEIR ANCESTORS!

CAN YOU SUGGEST ANYTHING, FATHER?

YES, MY BOY, I CAN. I'VE DECIDED TO MAKE A SPEECH TO THE VILLAGERS OPPOSITE. THAT'LL BRIDGE THE GAP. THEY'LL SOON SEE HOW WRONG THEY WERE TO DITCH ME!

AND IN CHIEF MAJESTIX'S HUT...

OH, FATHER, DO YOU REMEMBER HOW HAPPY THE VILLAGE WAS WHEN WE ONLY HAD ONE CHIEF, ALTRUISTIX?

YES, I DO! THE OLD SO-AND-SO TOOK AFTER HIS COUSIN ALCAPONIX... MAKING OFF WITH ALL THE VILLAGE'S TAXES!

THIS IS ALL THAT FOOL CLEVERDIX'S FAULT! HE STOLE VOTES WHICH WERE MINE BY RIGHT.

HE EVEN PROMISED TO BRING DOWN INFLATION, AND THOSE IDIOTS FELL FOR IT! THAT WAS WHEN THE BALLOON WENT UP!

MELODRAMA IS RIGHT! WE NEED A SINGLE CHIEF TO LEAD THE VILLAGE. YOU LET THEM KNOW OVER ON THE LEFT THAT YOU'RE THE RIGHTFUL CHIEF!

CODFIX, YOUR ADVICE ISN'T ALWAYS CODSWALLOP! YES, I'LL ADDRESS THEM!

AND SOON AFTERWARDS...

7

BROTHERS, WE ARE HOVERING ON THE BRINK OF VILLAGE DISASTER! BUT THE PARTY OF THE LEFT OFFERS FULL EMPLOYMENT...MAXIMUM PRODUCTIVE POTENTIAL FOR ALL WORKERS...

...SHIELD-BEARERS INCLUDED. DON'T YOU LISTEN TO MAJESTIX! HE'D PLUCK THE VERY WINGS FROM YOUR HELMETS! WORKERS OF THE VILLAGE, UNITE!

CROSS THE GREAT DIVIDE!

POPULAR OPINION HAS REPLIED IN THE ONLY FITTING WAY TO THE LYING INSINUATIONS OF THAT DOUBLE-DEALING CLEVERDIX! WITH HIS BRINKMANSHIP, HE'D HAPPILY SACRIFICE THE GOOD OF THE VILLAGE TO THE INTERESTS OF ROME, SPOUTING HOT AIR ON BEHALF OF THE ROMAN GEEZER*...

*JULIUS CAESAR

FRIENDS, GAULS, COUNTRYMEN, LET US THROW IN OUR LOT TOGETHER!

COME TO MY...

VERY WELL, LET'S FIGHT IT OUT, YOU ROTTEN LOT, AND WE'LL SEE WHO'S LEFT IN COMMAND!

BY ALL MEANS, AND WE'LL SEE YOU DO A RIGHT ABOUT TURN!

RSPRRRR! RSPRRR!

ELSEWHERE, PEACE IS REIGNING IN ANOTHER LITTLE VILLAGE, A VILLAGE WE ALL KNOW WELL...

LOOK, IF PEACE IS REIGNING IN OUR LITTLE VILLAGE, THE VILLAGE THEY ALL KNOW WELL, THAT MEANS THE ROMANS ARE SULKING, ASTERIX!

NO, OBELIX, IT JUST MEANS THEY'VE LEARNT A BIT OF SENSE!

?!

WHAT ARE YOU DOING ON THAT CONTRAPTION, O CHIEF VITAL-STATISTIX?

ER...WELL...I'M GOING OUT SHOPPING FOR IMPEDIMENTA. SHE'S FEELING A BIT UNDER THE WEATHER.

BUT WHAT'S THE CART FOR?

OH, THE CART! THAT'S A NEW IDEA OF MINE. IT MEANS THESE CLUMSY GREAT OAFS CAN'T LET ME DOWN ANY MORE WHEN THE FANCY TAKES THEM.

RIGHT, YOU TWO! WHATEVER YOU DO NOW, I STAND FIRM ON MY TRUSTY SHIELD! SO OFF WE GO SHOPPING!

!

BONG!

SIGH

AND HE CAN'T SHOP US FOR THAT, OR GET NEW SHIELD-BEARERS...

NO, WE SHIELD-BEARERS OPERATE A CLOSED SHOP!

DOWNCAST AGAIN, PIGGYWIGGY? THINKING YOURSELF SO CLEVER... HUH! PIGS MIGHT FLY!

DINNER'S READY!

DINNER'S READY!

DINNER'S READY!

DINNER'S READY!

DINNER'S READY!

DINNER'S READY!

DINNER'S READY!

DINNER'S READY!

LISTEN, WHY DON'T WE CARRY ON LATER TO HELP OUR DINNER DOWN?

AND MEANWHILE, WOULD YOU MIND HELPING *ME* DOWN? MY WIFE'S WAITING!

THESE FISH ARE ALMOST PAST IT, EVEN FOR HELPING PEOPLE RELAX. CHANGE AND DECAY IN ALL AROUND I SEE...

NIGHT HAS FALLEN, AND ALL IS CALM AGAIN IN THE VILLAGE.

TIME FOR BED, SCHIZO-PHRENIX!

COMING, DARLING!

BONG!

CODFIX IS GOING TO ASK THE ROMANS TO HELP MAKE MY FATHER CHIEF OF THE WHOLE VILLAGE...AND IN RETURN MY FATHER HAS PROMISED HIM MY HAND IN MARRIAGE!

HOW DARE HE?! BUT I'M FROM THE OPPOSITE CAMP, MELODRAMA...WHY ARE YOU TELLING ME ALL THIS?

BECAUSE YOU'RE THE ONLY PERSON WITH ANY SENSE IN THIS CRAZY VILLAGE, AND I DON'T WANT TO MARRY COD-FIX! O HISTRIONIX, HISTRIONIX! WHERE-FORE ART THOU HISTRIONIX?

?

!?!

RAISE THE ALARM!

BONK!

ARE YOU HURT, HISTRIONIX?

NO, I'M ALL RIGHT... I FANCY A PASSING SHOAL OF FISH BROKE MY FALL!

14

MY OWN DAUGHTER IN LEAGUE WITH THE ENEMY! TREACHERY UNDER MY OWN ROOF!

AND MY OWN FATHER ISN'T ASHAMED TO ASK THE ROMANS FOR HELP IN FIGHTING OUR OWN FRIENDS AND RELATIONS!

SHUT UP, YOU UNGRATEFUL CHILD! I'M GOING TO LOCK YOU IN YOUR ROOM, AND YOU DON'T COME OUT UNTIL THE DAY YOU MARRY CODFIX!

I NEVER WILL! I'D RATHER BE A VIRGIN SERVING VESTA* ALL MY LIFE!

*GIRLS CURRIED FAVOUR WITH THIS GODDESS

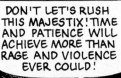

DON'T LET'S RUSH THIS MAJESTIX! TIME AND PATIENCE WILL ACHIEVE MORE THAN RAGE AND VIOLENCE EVER COULD!

SOMETIMES I WONDER HOW I THINK THESE THINGS UP...

O LOVELY MELODRAMA, PLEASE ACCEPT THIS PRETTY BUNCH OF FLOWERS!

WHAT MAKES YOU THINK YOU'RE A SMASH HIT WITH ME?

MEANWHILE...

FATHER, WAKE UP!

HMPH? WHAT IS IT?

MAJESTIX AND HIS HENCHMAN CODFIX ARE PLANNING TO ASK THE ROMANS TO HELP THEM CONQUER THE WHOLE VILLAGE!

OH, ARE THEY? WELL, SON, I WANT YOU TO GO IN SEARCH OF MY OLD COMRADE-IN-ARMS VITALSTATISTIX. HE AND I FOUGHT TOGETHER AT GERGOVIA...

HE'S CHIEF OF A ARMORICAN VILLAGE A FEW DAYS' JOURNEY AWAY. THANKS TO THE DRUID GETAFIX'S MAGIC POTION, HE HAS KEPT THE WHOLE MIGHT OF CAESAR'S LEGIONS AT BAY! EXPLAIN IT ALL TO HIM, AND TELL HIM I NEED HIS HELP!

IN THE ROMAN CAMP NEAR THE DIVIDED VILLAGE...

HEY, SOURPUS, I'LL SWAP YOU TWO SENTRY DUTIES FOR ONE LAUNDRY FATIGUE!

NOTHING DOING! YOU ALREADY OWE ME THREE COOK-HOUSE FATIGUES AND TWO LATRINE FATIGUES!

BACK AT THE RECRUITMENT OFFICE, THEY TOLD US WE'D GET BEAUTIFUL SLAVE-GIRLS FROM THE COUNTRIES WE CONQUERED...

BACK IN ROME, CAESAR SAID HE WAS COUNTING ON US TO CLEAN UP THE BARBARIANS...WHAT A WASH-OUT!

LOOT, THEY SAID. THE CARROT FOR THE DONKEY!

IT'S A MAN'S LIFE IN THE ARMY, THEY SAID...

ALL RIGHT, WE KNOW, WE KNOW!

DECURION INFECTIUS VIRUS, THIS TENT IS A PIGSTY, AND THE COOKING IN THE CAMP IS GOING FROM BAD TO WORSE!

I KNOW. THE COOKHOUSE IS RE-VOLTING, O CENTURION UMBRAGEOUS CUMULONIMBUS. THERE'S A MOOD OF GENERAL UNREST. THE MEN WANT SLAVES TO DO THE DIRTY WORK, BUT CAESAR SAID WE WEREN'T TO TAKE SLAVES DURING THE ROMAN PEACE!

WISH I'D BROUGHT MY SLAVEGIRL FROM HOME...NICE LITTLE ROMAN PIECE*, SHE IS!

* PAX ROMANA

(14A)

CENTURION, I HAVE THE ANSWER TO ALL YOUR PROBLEMS!

?!

WHO LET YOU INTO THIS CAMP, GAUL?

THE MAN ON DUTY AT THE GATE. HE WAS QUITE HAPPY WHEN I OFFERED HIM A SLAVE IN EXCHANGE!

WHO ARE YOU, ANYWAY? HOW DARE YOU CORRUPT MY LEGIONARIES?

I'M FROM MAJESTIX, RIGHT-FUL CHIEF OF THE RIGHT SIDE OF OUR VILLAGE. I'M HIS ALTER EGO AND RIGHT HAND!

TOK TOK

AND THIS IS MY LEFT FOOT! BE OFF, OR IT'LL ALTER YOUR EGO!

CHIEF MAJESTIX WANTS YOU TO HELP HIM PUT DOWN A REBELLION LED BY CLEVERDIX!

THAT'S NONE OF MY BUSINESS! THIS IS YOUR NUNC DIMITTIS...GET OUT, OR YOU'LL BE SINGING A DIFFERENT TUNE. A FUNERAL DIRGE FROM HYMNS ANCIENT*!

*HYMNS MODERN AS YET UNWRITTEN

(14B)

19

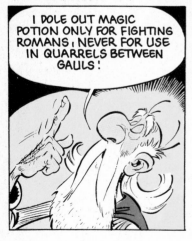

20

YOU KNOW, FATHER, MAJESTIX REALLY DID ACT IN A MANNER WORTHY OF A CHIEF!

ALL THINGS CONSIDERED, I MUST ADMIT HE CARRIED IT OFF IN STYLE!

WE'LL GET THEM THIS TIME, ASTERIX!!!

NO, OBELIX! IT COULD PUT MAJESTIX AND HIS WARRIORS IN DANGER!

A LITTLE LATER...

DON'T WORRY, MELODRAMA! IF MY FATHER WILL AGREE, WE'LL ORGANIZE A CAMPAIGN AGAINST THE ROMANS TO FREE OUR FELLOW VILLAGERS!

WE MUST DO SOMETHING, HISTRIONIX!

I CERTAINLY AGREE! MAJESTIX MAY BE MY OPPONENT, BUT I DON'T WANT HIM USING HIS SACRIFICE AS AN ARGUMENT AT THE POLLS!

HUH!

WAIT A MOMENT! I'VE GOT A BETTER IDEA!

THE ROMANS OF THESE PARTS DON'T KNOW GETAFIX, OBELIX AND ME. WE'LL GO TO THE ROMAN CAMP ON OUR OWN. IF IT'S SLAVES THEY WANT, WE'LL APPLY FOR THE JOB, AND SET THE PRISONERS FREE!

AN EXCELLENT IDEA, ASTERIX!

OOH, YES! GOODY, GOODY, GOODY! A CHANCE TO SAMPLE THE LOCAL ROMANS AT LAST...

CLAP! CLAP! CLAP!

...THUMPING ROMANS IS LIKE HAVING DINNER: IT'S NICE TO EAT OUT FOR A CHANGE!

IN THE ROMAN CAMP...

WE WILL NEVER BE YOUR SLAVES, ROMAN!

DO YOU KNOW THE PENALTIES FOR A SLAVES' REVOLT? YOU'D BETTER STOP AND THINK, UNLESS YOU WANT TO MAKE THE LIONS IN THE CIRCUS MAXIMUS AT ROME A SQUARE MEAL!

AND WHILE THEY'RE THINKING, CHAIN THEM ALL UP WELL!!!

CAN I HAVE THOSE THREE SENTRY DUTIES BACK? THE ONES YOU SWAPPED FOR MY COOKHOUSE FATIGUE!

PRICES HAVE RISEN... IT'LL BE FOUR SENTRY DUTIES NOW!

MEANWHILE...

GOOD LUCK, FRIENDS!

DON'T WORRY, MELODRAMA! THANKS TO GETAFIX'S KNOW-HOW, OBELIX'S STRENGTH, DOGMATIX'S NOSE AND MY CUNNING, WE'LL SOON HAVE YOUR FATHER HOME!

FUNNY HOW SURE OF THEMSELVES CLEVERDIX'S ALLIES SEEM! I'LL FOLLOW THE AT A SAFE DISTANCE!

DOGMATIX HAS BEEN SNIFFING ABOUT EVER SINCE WE LEFT! I THINK HE'S PICKED UP THE SCENT OF A BOAR!

NO, NO, IT'S JUST A RED HERRING.

IF SO, IT'S BEEN TAKING CODLIVER OIL!

SNIFF! SNIFF!

RIGHT, YOU GET THE IDEA, OBELIX? WE'RE HUMBLE SLAVES, SO NO THUMPING THE ROMANS!

LISTEN, ASTERIX...

...IS THERE SUCH A THING AS A SLAVE-DOG?

24

THE GODS MUST HAVE SENT YOU, GAUL! A SPOT OF GOOD COOKING WILL CERTAINLY MAKE A CHANGE FROM THE USUAL MESS!

OH, WE CAN COOK A GOOD MEAL FOR ALL YOUR MEN, CENTURION! THE FEAST OF THE CENTURY, AS YOU MIGHT SAY!

FOR STARTERS, A FORTIFYING SOUP. THE MEAT COURSE... A REALLY NICE CUT! SAY CHUMP CHOP, STEWED IN YOUR... I MEAN, IN ITS OWN JUICE. AND WE WON'T MAKE A HASH OF IT. IF YOU FANCY POULTRY, WE CAN COOK YOUR GOOSE FOR YOU! GAME FOR ANYTHING? THEN GROUSE AND QUAIL. AFTER THAT, YOU GET YOUR DESSERTS: A FOOL, WELL BEATEN, PERHAPS SOME INSTANT WHIP, AND A FEW RASPBERRIES. ALL WASHED DOWN WITH THE GAULISH BEER WE CALL WALLOP... IT PACKS QUITE A PUNCH!

THAT'LL DO FINE! GET ON WITH IT... I CAN HARDLY WAIT!

WE SHAN'T TAKE LONG!

WINK!

LOOK HERE, GETAFIX, WHY DON'T WE ADD A FEW NICE ROAST BOARS?

?!? WHY NOT GO AND CHOP UP SOME KINDLING FOR THE FIRE, OBELIX?

WELL, I ONLY THOUGHT HE'D GONE AND FORGOTTEN THE BOARS...

!

CHOP! CHOP! CHOP! CHOP!

AMAZING! I'VE NEVER SEEN ANYONE CHOP WOOD LIKE THAT BEFORE!

OH, THAT'S NOTHING! I COULD CUT A WHOLE TREE DOWN THAT WAY, ONLY DOGMATIX WOULDN'T LIKE IT!

SOON AFTERWARDS...

READY IN A MOMENT!

I'M A BIT WORRIED, CENTURION! A COUSIN OF MINE STATIONED IN ARMORICA TOLD ME ABOUT A DRUID THE WHO HAS STRANGE POWERS, AND I'M JUST WONDERING WHETHER...

YOU'VE GOT A POINT, INFECTIUS VIRUS. WE MUST BE CAREFUL!

WOULD YOU LIKE TO TASTE THE SOUP FOR SEASONING, CENTURION?

JUST A MOMENT, GAUL! HOW DO I KNOW YOU'RE NOT TRYING TO POISON THE GARRISON, SO AS TO SET THE PRISONERS FREE?

I QUITE UNDERSTAND YOUR FEELINGS. YOU DON'T WANT TO FIND YOURSELF IN THE SOUP. SO WE'LL DRINK SOME OURSELVES, TO SHOW IT'S ALL RIGHT!

AND TO PROVE IT EVEN MORE CONCLUSIVELY, WE'LL GIVE SOME TO THE PRISONERS TOO!

NO, OBELIX NOT YOU!

AND WHY NOT HIM?

YES, WHY NOT ME?

BECAUSE HE FELL INTO THE CAULDRON WHEN HE WAS A BABY, AND... ER... UM...

AND HE HAS TO STAY ON A STRICT DIET FOR THE GOOD OF HIS MENTAL HEALTH, THAT'S WHY NOT HIM!

DON'T WORRY, WE'RE HERE TO RESCUE YOU. THE POTION WILL GIVE YOU THE STRENGTH YOU NEED. WATCH FOR OUR SIGNAL! THEN YOU HAVE NOTHING TO LOSE BUT YOUR CHAINS!

SOON AFTERWARDS...

YOU SEE, ROMAN, THE WAS NO NEED FOR YOU TO WORRY!

WELL, SINCE THERE ISN'T ANY SOUP LEFT, LET'S GO STRAIGHT ON TO THE NEXT COURSE ON THE MENU, WHICH IS...

THE CHOP!

THE MENU! I SEE IT ALL NOW!!!

SO DO WE! COME ON, MEN!

SNAP!

28

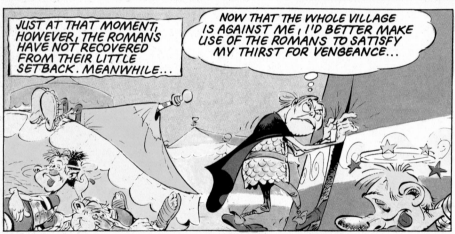

RIGHT! WE SHALL NOW FORGET THIS WHOLE UNFORTUNATE EPISODE AND CLEAR UP THE MESS! I WANT THE GARRISON ALL SPRUCED UP AND LOOKING LIKE A CENA CANIS*! DISMISS!

*LATIN: DOG'S DINNER

WHAT'S CENA CANIS?

DOG LATIN, YOU IDIOT!

AH, A NICE GOBLET OF WINE WILL HELP ME FORGET MY TROUBLES!

GLUG! GLUG! GLUG!

AAAH! BY JUPITER, I'M FEELING ON TOP OF THE WORLD!

?!? WHO ARE YOU, GAUL, AND WHO LET YOU INTO THIS CAMP?

IT'S WORKING!

I'VE COME TO WARN YOU, O CENTURION! THE GAULS OF THE NEARBY VILLAGE HAVE BROKEN THE PAX ROMANA! THEY'VE BASHED UP YOUR LEGIONARIES AND RANSACKED YOUR CAMP!

IMPOSSIBLE! OR ARE YOU GIVING ME SOME INSIDE DOPE?

O CUMULONIMBUS, THE MEN DON'T WANT TO CLEAR UP THE MESS! THEY'RE ALL REPORTING SICK!

SICK BAY

AND LATER...

I STILL HAVE NO IDEA WHO YOU ARE, GAUL, BUT YOU WON'T FIND ME UNGRATEFUL FOR SERVICES RENDERED!

WE CAN TALK ABOUT THAT LATER, ONCE YOU'VE DONE FOR THE VILLAGE AND ALL ITS INHABITANTS.

BUT WATCH OUT! THERE'S A DRUID WITH THEM, AND HE HAS A POTION WHICH MAKES ANYONE WHO DRINKS IT INVINCIBLE!

CENTURION, A COUSIN OF MINE STATIONED IN ARMORICA TOLD ME ABOUT A DRUID THERE WHO HAS STRANGE POWERS, AND I'M JUST WONDERING WHETHER...

YOU'VE GOT A POINT, INFECTIUS VIRUS! WE MUST BE CAREFUL!

MEANWHILE, IN THE GAULISH VILLAGE...

THE MAGIC POTION'S READY. WE'D BETTER PUT IT SAFE ON NEUTRAL GROUND SOMEWHERE WHILE WE WAIT TO SEE IF THE ROMANS ARE COMING BACK!

SCHIZOPHRENIX'S HUT IS NEUTRAL GROUND. IT'S BANG IN THE MIDDLE OF THE VILLAGE.

YES, LET'S PUT IT THERE. THAT FOOL SCHIZOPHRENIX HAS NEVER BEEN ABLE TO DECIDE WHICH SIDE HE'S ON!

DIDN'T YOU EVER THINK OF PUTTING FLOOR-BOARDS DOWN OVER THE GAP?

THAT'S FLOORED HIM! WE'LL DO IT NOW.

AND SO, A LITTLE LATER...

I'LL WATCH OVER THE CAULDRON TONIGHT, TO MAKE DOUBLY SURE!

THEN YOU'D BETTER HAVE THIS GOURD OF MAGIC POTION, ASTERIX. YOU NEVER KNOW, YOU MIGHT NEED A BOOSTER DOSE, IN SPITE OF THE POTION IN THE CAULDRON.

AND THAT NIGHT, ON THE OUTSKIRTS OF THE WOOD NEAR THE GAULISH VILLAGE...

I DON'T TRUST THAT DRUID AND HIS SECRET WEAPONS! I THINK I'D BETTER GO SCOUTING AHEAD BEFORE WE ATTACK!

AND WHATEVER YOU DO, DON'T MOVE TILL I GET BACK!

RIGHT, BUT HURRY UP! I CAN'T WAIT TO GET MY REVENGE ON THOSE GAULS!

THE GODS OF THE UNDERWORLD ARE ON MY SIDE! IT'S THAT FOOL CONGENITAL-IDIOTIX ON SENTRY DUTY! I'LL SOON DEAL WITH HIM!

HALT! WHO GOES THERE?

IT'S ME. CODFIX.

I MIGHT HAVE KNOWN FROM THE SMELL! WHAT DO YOU WANT?

I WANT TO ASK CHIEF MAJESTIX TO FORGIVE ME!

YOU CAN COME IN, BUT IF I WERE YOU I'D KEEP MY DISTANCE FROM MAJESTIX!

WHY ARE YOU MOUNTING GUARD LIKE THIS? WHAT ARE YOU AFRAID OF?

WE'RE AFRAID THE ROMANS MAY COME BACK. BUT LUCKILY GETAFIX THE DRUID HAS MADE US SOME OF HIS MAGIC POTION. IT'S SAFE IN SCHIZO-PHRENIX'S HUT!

TEEHEE!

I'VE NEVER BEEN ABLE TO SEE STARS INSIDE A HUT BEFORE!

BONG!

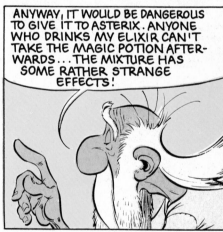

BLAM!

BONG!

THESE ROMANS ARE REALLY CRAZY! THEY'RE NOT AT THE CIRCUS NOW!

AND MEANWHILE...

BING!

BANG!

BONG!

AHA! NO MORE GLOBE-TROTTING! WE'RE BACK TO NORMAL!

PICK UP YOUR WEAPONS AND GET BACK TO BATTLE STATIONS!!!

O CUMULONIMBUS, I'M AN OLD SOLDIER, AND I'VE BEEN AROUND, BUT I'VE NEVER FOUGHT IN TERRAIN QUITE LIKE THIS!

I'LL TELL YOU ANOTHER FUNNY THING... WE'VE LOST SIGHT OF THE ENEMY!

BUT WE'RE STILL HERE, O ROMAN!

?!?

EEEEK!

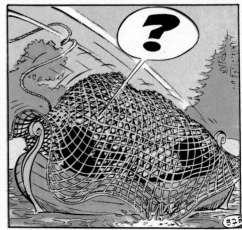

43

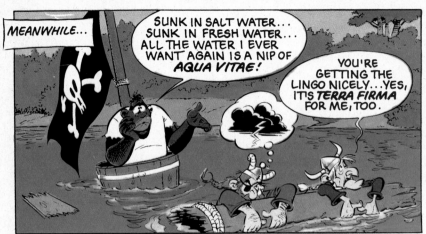

MEANWHILE...

SUNK IN SALT WATER... SUNK IN FRESH WATER... ALL THE WATER I EVER WANT AGAIN IS A NIP OF *AQUA VITAE!*

YOU'RE GETTING THE LINGO NICELY...YES, IT'S *TERRA FIRMA* FOR ME, TOO.

QUICK, LET'S GO AND SET MAJESTIX'S MIND AT REST!

IN TIMES OF TROUBLE SUCH AS THIS, IT IS ONLY RIGHT TO FORGET OUR DIFFERENCES, AND I FEEL FOR YOU, MAJESTIX!

THEY'RE BACK, WITH MELODRAMA!

OH, FATHER, HISTRIONIX ACTED LIKE A TRUE CHIEF!

I'M EXTREMELY GRATEFUL TO HISTRIONIX FOR HIS BRAVE ACTION, BUT THAT'S GOING A BIT TOO FAR, MY DEAR!

OH NO, IT ISN'T. AFTER ALL, HISTRIONIX IS THE SON OF A CHIEF!

SON OF A CHIEF MY FOOT!!! I'M THE ONLY REAL CHIEF AROUND HERE!

OH, FOR GOODNESS'SAKE, WE'VE HAD ENOUGH OF THIS! IF YOU MUST FIGHT FOR THE CHIEFTAINSHIP, KEEP IT BETWEEN THE TWO OF YOU!!!

?!

?!

MELODRAMA IS QUITE RIGHT! FIGHT IF YOU MUST, BUT LEAVE THE OTHER VILLAGERS OUT OF IT. THEY'VE HAD ENOUGH OF YOUR QUARRELS!

AND SOON AFTERWARDS...

NOW, YOU SENILE OLD DOTARD, I'LL SHOW YOU WHAT A REAL CHIEF CAN DO, AND WITH MY BARE HANDS!

YOU DYSPEPTIC OLD FOGY! YOU'RE IN FOR A SHOCK!

YOU'LL NEED A NEUTRAL UMPIRE. I VOLUNTEER TO REFEREE YOUR SINGLE COMBAT!

ACCORDING TO THE RULES, THE FIGHT MAY GO ON UNTIL SUNRISE TOMORROW. THE LOSER IS THE MAN WHO STAYS DOWN AFTER A COUNT OF 100! OFF YOU GO, AND MAY THE BEST MAN WIN THE PRIZE!

BONK!

CLONK!

V SESTERTII ON CLEVERDIX!

X ON MAJESTIX!

XV ON CLEVERDIX!

AS EVENING COMES ON, MANY OF THE AUDIENCE, TIRING OF THE SHOW, LEAVE THE RING.

THEY OUGHT TO REVISE THE RULES OF THESE PRIZEFIGHTS.

IT'S LATE. I'M GOING TO BED, ASTERIX!

YAAAWN! SO ARE WE. DOGMATIX AND I DON'T TAKE MUCH INTEREST IN FIGHTS WHEN THERE AREN'T ANY ROMANS OR ANY BOARS.

ZZZZ!

EVEN ASTERIX IS UNABLE TO KEEP HIS EYES OPEN. ALL ALONE, IN THE MOONLIGHT, THE TWO CHIEFS ARE STILL EQUALLY MATCHED.

ZZZZZ!

AND AT SUNRISE...

COCKADOODLE-DO!

?!?

RRRRR!

ZZZZ!

FRIENDS, FATE HAS DECIDED THE RESULT OF THE SINGLE COMBAT... NO ONE HAS WON AND NO ONE HAS LOST!

BUT YOU CAN HAVE A YOUNG, STRONG CHIEF IF YOU CHOOSE HISTRIONIX TO LEAD YOU, AND MELODRAMA WILL MAKE A WISE AND BEAUTIFUL CHIEF'S WIFE!

HURRAH! LONG LIVE HISTRIONIX! LONG LIVE MELODRAMA!

?.!?

OH, WELL, I RATHER THINK ALL WE CAN DO IS GET DRESSED AGAIN!

YOU SAID IT, FAT-FACE!

REUNITED AT LAST, UNDER THE RULE OF THEIR NEW CHIEF HISTRIONIX, THE GAULS OF THE VILLAGE DIVERT PART OF THE NEARBY RIVER INTO THE DITCH, WHICH NO LONGER SERVES ANY USEFUL PURPOSE. AND NOW THERE IS NO PARTY OF THE RIGHT OR PARTY OF THE LEFT, ONLY A RIGHT BANK AND A LEFT BANK, RUNNING WATER ON EVERYONE'S DOORSTEP, AND FREEDOM FOR ALL THE VILLAGERS TO GO TO AND FRO.

THE BACK AND FORTH BRIDGE

THE CHILDREN CAN STILL GATHER THE FRUITS OF OTHER PEOPLE'S LABOURS WITH IMPUNITY...

YOU'VE GOT NO RIGHT TO DO THAT! THAT'S MY TREE!!!

SCRUNCH!

A NEW AND PRACTICAL USE IS FOUND FOR THE TWO GATEWAYS OF THE VILLAGE. HERE YOU SEE THE FIRST ONE-WAY SYSTEM KNOWN TO ANCIENT HISTORY.

AND SCHIZOPHRENIX'S HUT IS REBUILT AT LAST... THOUGH THE ARCHITECTS DID SLIP UP HERE AND THERE IN THEIR PLANS.

SPLOSH!

ANY IDEA WHAT BECAME OF THAT SCOUNDREL CODFIX?

NO, BUT I SHOULDN'T BE SURPRISED IF HE WAS STILL UP TO DIRTY WORK.

SURE ENOUGH, IN THE ROMAN CAMP...

WELL, SLAVE, HAVE YOU DONE THOSE VEGETABLES YET?

AND THE LAUNDRY? AND DON'T FORGET THE IRONING!

THE WEDDING OF MELODRAMA AND HISTRIONIX IS CELEBRATED AMIDST REJOICINGS FOR ALL AND BOARS FOR SOME.

SCRUNCH! SCRUNCH!

SCRUNCH! SCRUNCH!

THE TIME COMES TO SAY GOODBYE.

HOW CAN WE EVER THANK YOU FOR ALL WE OWE YOU?

YOU'RE HAPPY, AND THAT'S ALL THE THANKS WE NEED!

HUH!

The End

PRINTED IN BELGIUM BY
proost
INTERNATIONAL BOOK PRODUCTION